Dear Parent:
Your child's love of reading starts here!

Every child learns to read in a different way and at his or her own speed. Some go back and forth between reading levels and read favorite books again and again. Others read through each level in order. You can help your young reader improve and become more confident by encouraging his or her own interests and abilities. From books your child reads with you to the first books he or she reads alone, there are I Can Read Books for every stage of reading:

My First

SHARED READING
Basic language, word repetition, and whimsical illustrations, ideal for sharing with your emergent reader

BEGINNING READING
Short sentences, familiar words, and simple concepts for children eager to read on their own

READING WITH HELP
Engaging stories, longer sentences, and language play for developing readers

3

READING ALONE
Complex plots, challenging vocabulary, and high-interest topics for the independent reader

I Can Read Books have introduced children to the joy of reading since 1957. Featuring award-winning authors and illustrators and a fabulous cast of beloved characters, I Can Read Books set the standard for beginning readers.

A lifetime of discovery begins with the magical words **"I Can Read!"**

Visit www.icanread.com for information on enriching your child's reading experience.

To all those who love ladybugs and
to Stephanie for the cutest ladybug ever.
—K.G.

To Kallie for seeing a story
in a ladybug drawing.
—S.F.C.

Dot the Ladybug: Dot Day

For information address HarperCollins Children's Books, a division of HarperCollins Publishers,
195 Broadway, New York, NY 10007.
www.icanread.com

Library of Congress Control Number: 2022948036
ISBN 978-0-06-313747-9 (trade bdg.)—ISBN 978-0-06-313746-2 (pbk.)

Book design by Marisa Rother

23 24 25 26 27 LB 10 9 8 7 6 5 4 3 2 1 First Edition

DOT THE LADYBUG

Dot Day

By KALLIE GEORGE
Pictures by STEPHANIE FIZER COLEMAN

HARPER
An Imprint of HarperCollins*Publishers*

Dot is a ladybug.
She likes dots.
A lot.

Ice cream dots.

Polka dots.

Dot-to-dots.

Dot is always spotting dots.

Here, with Spots.

There, with Jots.
Dot spots lots every day.

Today is a BIG day.
It's her Dot Day.

One,

two,

three,

four,

five.

Dot has five dots.
And she is five!

It's time for a party.

But where are Dot's friends?

Dot can’t spot anyone.

Not here.

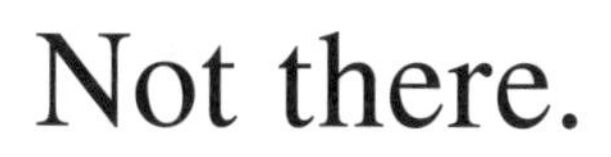

Not there.

Not anywhere.

They forgot about Dot.

What's this?

A funny dot.

A drippy dot.

“Hmmm . . . it’s a mystery.”

Dot follows the dots. . . .

One, two, three,
four, five.

Dot spots . . .

. . . her friends!

"Hello, Dot!"

“Hello, friends.”

Dot solved the mystery.

Happy Dot Day!

Everyone plays stick-
the-dot-on-the-spot.

They eat a cake
with sprinkle spots.
And Dot gets a gift . . .

A Dot Spotter.
Perfect for spotting
more dots!

Dot loves dots and spots.
And spotting dots.
But most of all . . .

Dot loves her friends.

Lots and lots.